Spooky Spots

HAUNTED CEMETERIES

ASHLEY STORM

BLACK RABBIT BOOKS

Bolt is published by Black Rabbit Books
P.O. Box 3263, Mankato, Minnesota, 56002.
www.blackrabbitbooks.com

Marysa Storm, editor; Grant Gould, designer;
Omay Ayres, photo researcher

Library of Congress Cataloging-in-Publication Data
Names: Storm, Ashley, author.
Title: Haunted cemeteries / by Ashley Storm.
Description: Mankato, Minnesota : Black Rabbit Books, [2021] | Series: Bolt. Spooky spots | Includes bibliographical references and index. | Audience: Ages 8-12 | Audience: Grades 4-6 | Summary: "Invites readers to explore the mysteries of haunted cemeteries through closely leveled text and engaging infographics"– Provided by publisher.
Identifiers: LCCN 2019026675 (print) | LCCN 2019026676 (ebook) | ISBN 9781623102777 (hardcover) | ISBN 9781644663738 (paperback) | ISBN 9781623103712 (ebook) | Subjects: LCSH: Haunted cemeteries–Juvenile literature. | Haunted places–Juvenile literature.
Classification: LCC BF1474.3 .S76 2021 (print) | LCC BF1474.3 (ebook) | DDC 133.1/22-dc23
LC record available at https://lccn.loc.gov/2019026675
LC ebook record available at https://lccn.loc.gov/2019026676

Printed in the United States. 2/20

Image Credits

Age Fotostock: CSP_ESchweitzer, 32; miss_j, 25; Alamy: Chronicle, 20–21; North Wind Picture Archives, 18; Samantha Ohlsen, 12; iStock: D-Keine, 4–5; Marilyn Nieves, 15; Museum of London: Henry Grant, 22 (inset); Shutterstock: AlexLMX, 26 (btm); Fer Gregory, Cover; Gary Perkin, 22 (bkgd); Gavin Swonnell, 6; Hitdelight, 10–11 (bkgd), 16–17; Hollygraphic, 29; Michal Sanca, 10–11 (shadow); mipan, 26 (top); Noel V. Baebler, 14–15; Odette Villarreal, 3; Sandra Cunningham, 9; siart, 22 (eyes); Tartila, Cover, 31; tatui suwat, 1; Valentyna7, 27; Zakharchenko Anna, 10

CONTENTS

CHAPTER 1

A Creepy CEMETERY

It was late at night. A man drove past Resurrection Cemetery in Justice, Illinois. He saw a woman near the gates. She looked lost. The man stopped and offered her a ride. The woman got in the car. But after the man started driving, she **vanished**! Later, he drove past the same cemetery. He swore he saw the woman dancing around the graves!

45%
believe
55%
don't
believe

CHAPTER 2

What's GOING ON?

Many people tell spooky stories about cemeteries. Cemeteries are resting places for the dead. But are the dead resting in peace? Some people say ghosts haunt cemeteries. They tell stories about strange things there.

How Many Believe?

About 45% of Americans believe in ghosts.

Sights and Sounds

Believers say ghosts try to let the living know they're there. They say some ghosts try to be seen. The ghosts might appear as balls of light or mist. They might even look like people. Other ghosts cause noises. Some people say ghosts even speak.

People have experienced strange things in cemeteries around the world. Could they really be haunted?

Some people are **superstitious**. When passing cemeteries, they hold their breath to stay safe from ghosts.

SIGNS OF A GHOST?

People have experienced weird things in some cemeteries. Some people say they're signs of ghosts.

STRANGE FIGURES
COLD SPOTS

The catacombs' tunnels are about 200 miles (322 kilometers) long. Some sections are lined with bones.

CHAPTER 3

Exploring THE SPOTS

People talk about haunted cemeteries around the world. Catacombs are underground cemeteries. One of the most famous is in Paris, France. More than 6 million bodies are buried there. Some visitors say they've seen or felt ghosts. Stories say some visitors have entered and never left! Maybe they should have read the entrance's warning. It says, "Stop! This is the **empire** of death."

Bonaventure Cemetery

Stories say a girl haunts Bonaventure Cemetery in Georgia. Gracie Watson was six years old when she died. Her father was very sad. He marked her grave with a statue. It looks just like Watson did. Some visitors say the statue cries blood. Others report hearing a girl laughing. Some even say they've seen her ghost playing.

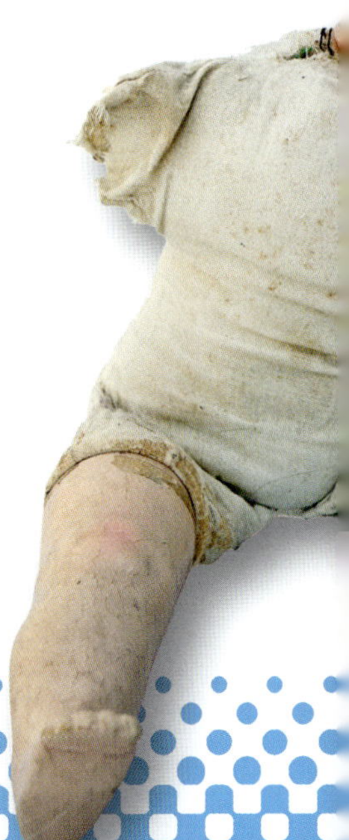

Some visitors leave toys for Watson's ghost.

WHERE ARE THEY?

This map shows where some haunted cemeteries might be found.

HIGHGATE CEMETERY
London, England
CATACOMBS
Paris, France

Howard Street Cemetery

A cemetery in Salem, Massachusetts, might be haunted by a witch! In 1692, people **accused** Giles Corey of witchcraft. He was killed in what's now Howard Street Cemetery. Before he died, Corey told the sheriff, "I **curse** you and Salem!" Today, some people believe his ghost appears before bad things happen. In 1914, a fire burned through Salem. People said they saw his ghost before the fire.

The Salem Witch Trials

Corey was killed for being a witch during the Salem Witch Trials. The Salem Witch Trials took place from 1692 to 1693 in Salem. During that time, people in Salem accused each other of being witches. Several people were **executed**. Like Corey, their ghosts might haunt Salem.

5
NUMBER OF PEOPLE WHO DIED IN JAIL

about 200
NUMBER OF PEOPLE ACCUSED

SALEM WITCH TRIALS BY THE NUMBERS

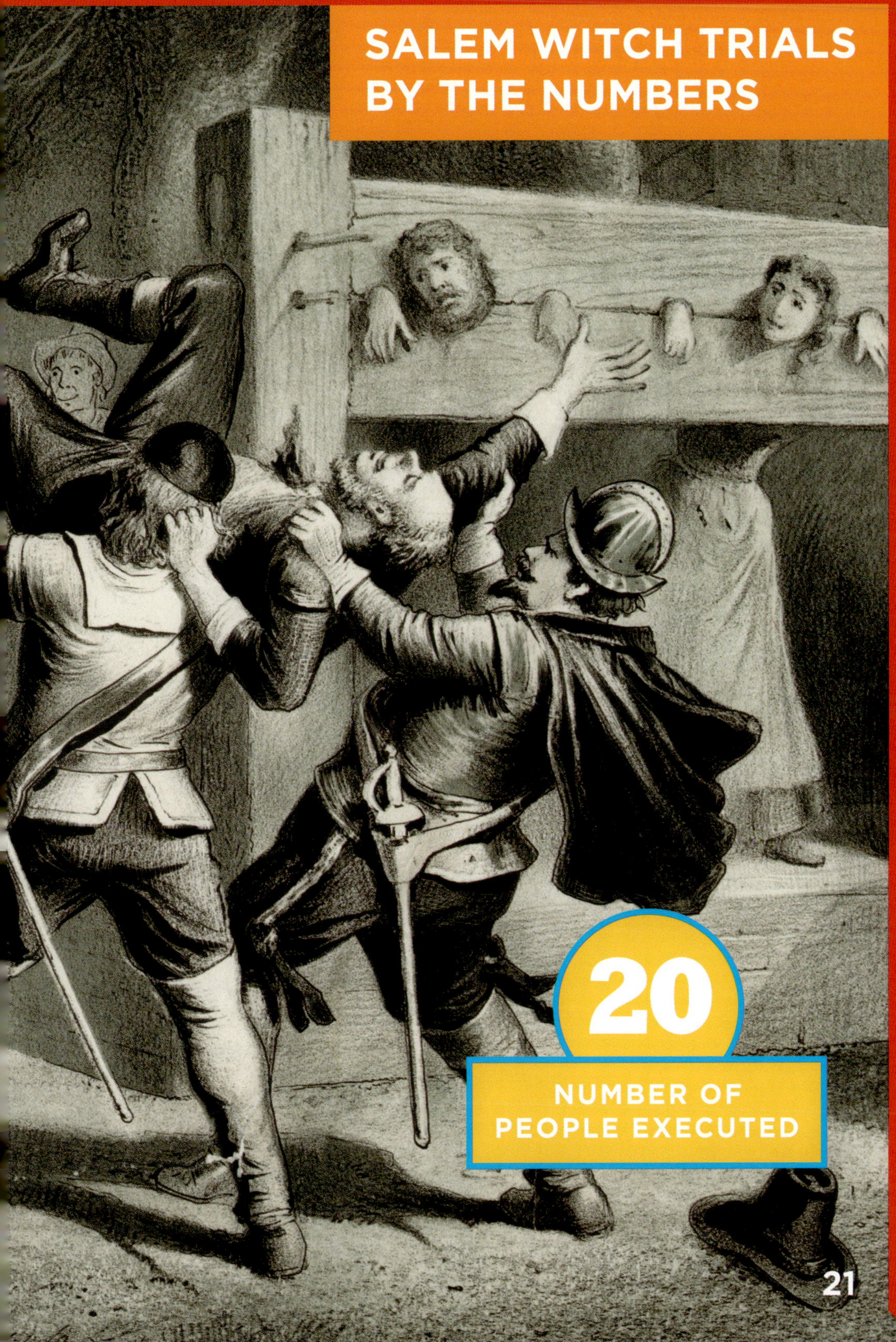

20

NUMBER OF PEOPLE EXECUTED

Highgate Cemetery

Highgate Cemetery is almost 200 years old. It might be haunted by many ghosts. People often talk about seeing a woman's ghost running around. Many believe a monster haunts it too. They call it the Highgate Vampire. People say it's tall. It has red eyes and a black robe. And it seems to vanish into thin air.

On March 13, 1970, people searched Highgate for the vampire. They did not find it.

CHAPTER 4

Are They REALLY HAUNTED?

Skeptics say ghosts are not real. They think some stories are made-up. They say others can be explained. A person's eyes can play tricks on them. Balls of light could be a car's headlights. Strange mist could just be fog. Weird noises could be animals. Wind can make places feel colder.

Ghost Hunting Tools

THERMOMETER

VIDEO CAMERA

RECORDER

Ghost Hunters

Ghost hunters search for ghosts. They go to cemeteries. There, they record sounds. They also take pictures. Sometimes the pictures show misty figures. Some recordings have strange noises. Some people say they prove ghosts exist. Others aren't so sure. They say pictures or sounds can be faked.

A Mystery

Cemeteries can feel creepy. After all, they are full of dead people. But are they really haunted? Nobody knows for sure.

GLOSSARY

accuse (uh-KYOOZ)—to blame for something wrong or illegal

curse (KURS)—to put someone under an evil spell meant to cause harm

empire (EM-pahyuhr)—a group of territories or peoples under one ruler

executed (EK-si-kyoo-td)—killed as punishment for a crime

skeptic (SKEP-tik)—a person who questions something

superstitious (soo-per-STISH-uhs)—showing or influenced by a belief or practice resulting from trust in magic or chance

vanish (VA-nish)—to disappear without explanation

LEARN MORE

BOOKS

Bodden, Valerie. *Cemeteries*. Creep Out. Mankato, MN: Creative Education, 2018.

Kovacs, Vic. *Haunted Churches and Graveyards.* Haunted or Hoax? New York: Crabtree Publishing Company, 2018.

Owings, Lisa. *Ghosts in Cemeteries.* Ghost Stories. Minneapolis: Bellwether Media, 2017.

WEBSITES

7 Spooky Things You Didn't Know about Ghosts
www.cbc.ca/kidscbc2/the-feed/monsters-101-all-about-ghosts

Haunted Cemeteries
www.scaryforkids.com/haunted-cemeteries/

Photo Tips: Trick Photography
kids.nationalgeographic.com/explore/photo-tips-trick-photography/

INDEX